JOY IN

WELCOME
to
MUDVILLE
est. 1827

MUDViLLE

written by
Bob Raczka

illustrations by
Glin Dibley

CAROLRHODA BOOKS • MINNEAPOLIS

Carolrhoda Books
A division of Lerner Publishing Group, Inc.
241 First Avenue North
Minneapolis, MN 55401 U.S.A.

Website address: www.lernerbooks.com

Library of Congress Cataloging-in-Publication Data

Raczka, Bob.
        Joy in Mudville / by Bob Raczka ; illustrated by Glin Dibley.
            p.   cm
        Summary: The day after Mighty Casey's strikeout, the Mudville Nine are in a
    crucial game when a relief pitcher—a girl—is sent in and quickly proves herself
    to the crowd using moves from football, tennis, and soccer.
        ISBN 978-0-7613-6015-5 (lib. bdg. : alk. paper)
        ISBN 978-1-4677-0953-8 (eBook)
        [1. Stories in rhyme. 2. Baseball—Fiction. 3. Sex role—Fiction. 4. Sports—
    Fiction.] I. Dibley, Glin, illustrator. II. Thayer, Ernest Lawrence, 1863–1940. Casey
    at the bat. III. Title.
    PZ8.3.R1155Joy 2014
    [E]—dc23   2013018619

Manufactured in the United States of America
1 - PC - 12/31/13

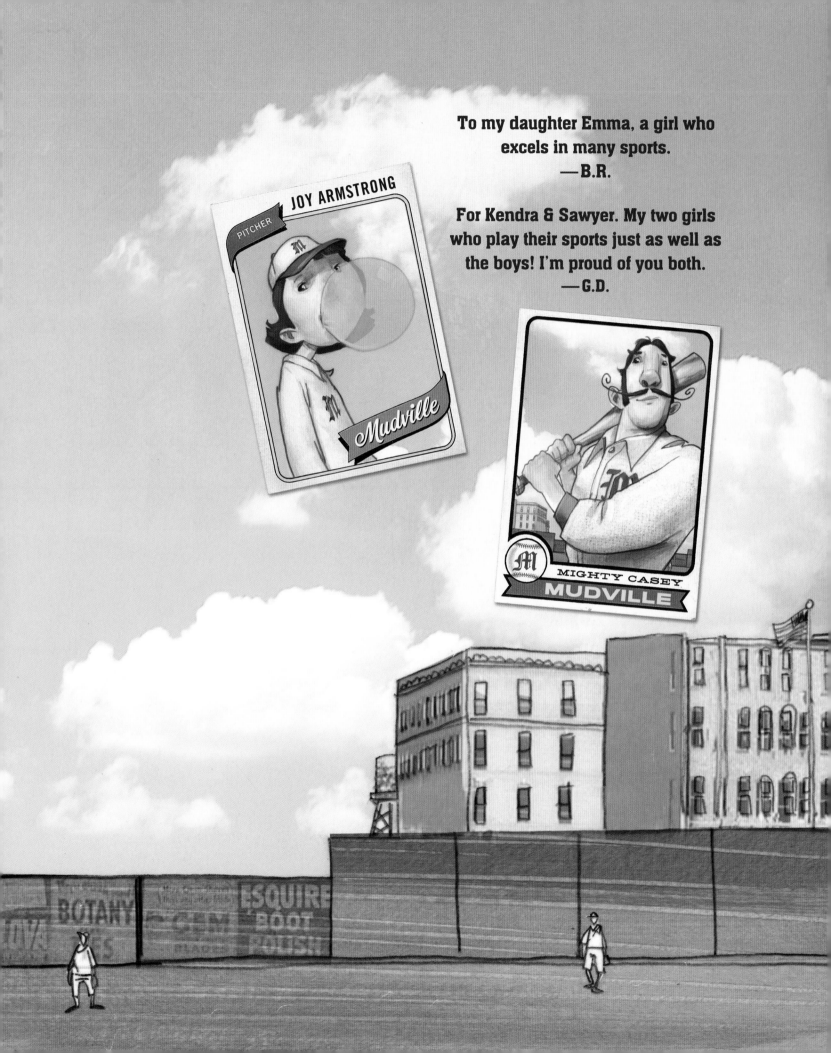

To my daughter Emma, a girl who
excels in many sports.
—B.R.

For Kendra & Sawyer. My two girls
who play their sports just as well as
the boys! I'm proud of you both.
—G.D.

He hoped it was a nightmare,
but when Mighty Casey woke,
The headline in the *Mudville Times*
read "**MIGHTY CASEY CHOKES.**"

The day before he'd struck out
with the tying runs on base,
And with the loss the Mudville Nine
fell into second place.

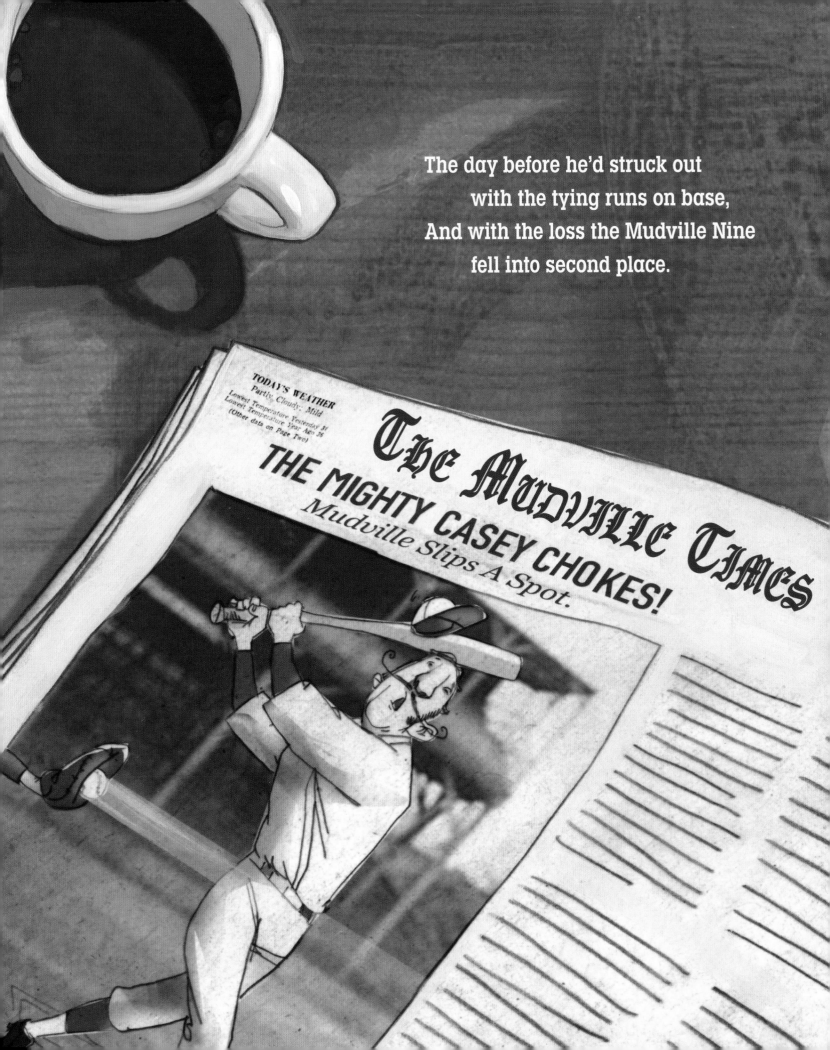

The next game was a crucial one
for Mudville's confidence,
And in the eighth they took the lead
when Casey cleared the fence.

But with two gone in inning nine,
their starter walked three straight.

The skipper sidled out and said,
"Sit down, kid. You did great."

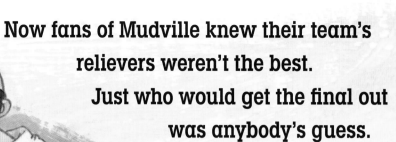

Now fans of Mudville knew their team's
relievers weren't the best.
Just who would get the final out
was anybody's guess.

The choice was this: a rookie
or a washed-up noodle arm.
The skipper played a hunch and
called on Joy, fresh off the farm.

As Joy, the rookie hurler,
took the mound to pitch relief,
Some twenty thousand fans
stared down in silent disbelief.

What struck them dumb
was not the unknown's anonymity.
It was the fact that Joy
(the rookie's first name) was a she.

Her hair was short and leather brown.
    Her eyes were grassy green.
And like a rack of fungo bats,
    her limbs were long and lean.
She used her spikes to groom the mound,
    then blew a big pink bubble,
As if to say, "I'm just the guy
    to pitch us out of trouble."

The crowd turned rude and booed,
but Joy pretended not to hear.
Deep down, she knew she'd have to
prove herself before they'd cheer.
Because she was a girl, the fans
assumed she'd come up short.
She'd show them soon enough that girls
excel in many sports.

Joy powwowed with her catcher
    'til they got their signals straight.
Then Jackson, fearsome slugger
    for their foes, approached the plate.

He smirked at Joy, but she stared past him,
    waiting for the sign.
Her catcher wagged one finger,
    just the pitch she had in mind.

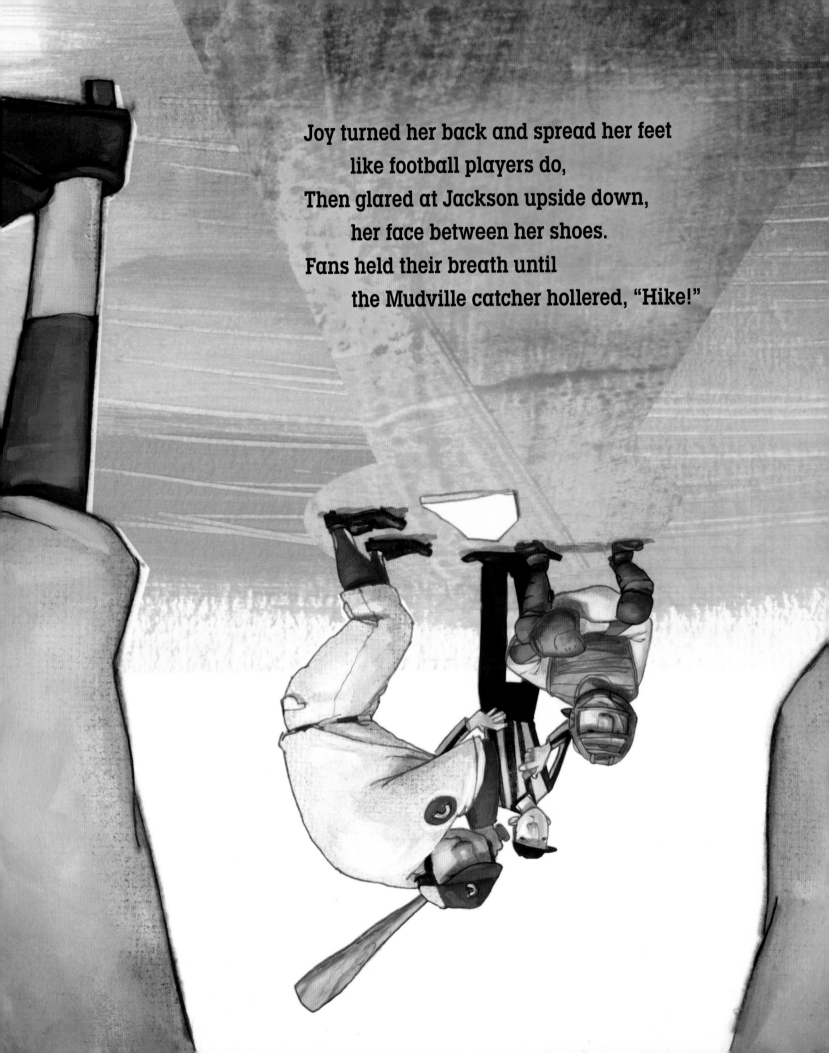

Joy turned her back and spread her feet
like football players do,
Then glared at Jackson upside down,
her face between her shoes.
Fans held their breath until
the Mudville catcher hollered, "Hike!"

Then like a shot, Joy snapped the ball
past Jackson for a strike.

Their faith restored, the crowd
resounded like a joyful choir.
They'd never seen a pitch like that,
so clever, so inspired.

"What is this, football?" Jackson growled,
    "I ain't no quarterback!"
The ump replied, "So far, you ain't
    no hitter either, Jack."

Her catcher dropped two fingers now;
Joy nodded, then she spit.

The smirk was gone from Jackson's face,
his eyes reduced to slits.

Then softly, like a tennis serve,
  Joy lobbed the ball up high
And smacked it homeward with her glove.

"**Strike two!**" the umpire cried.

A shock wave shook the ballpark as
the fickle fans went wild,
While Jackson stepped out of the box,
complaining like a child.

This time, her catcher flashed three fingers
    down between his knees,
While Jackson's knuckles turned bone white
    around the bat he squeezed.
Joy slowly chewed her gum
    and tugged her cap 'til it was straight,

Then dribbled once and launched
an arcing jump shot toward the plate.

What happened next caught Joy off guard—
    big Jackson turned to bunt.
He laid it down the third base line.
    It was the perfect stunt.

The man on third took off and
        barreled homeward at top speed,
Determined to erase
        the one-to-nothing Mudville lead.

Joy charged the ball but had no time
    to pick it up and throw.
So thinking fast, she kicked it soccer-style
    with her toe.
The ball arrived. The runner slid.
    A dust cloud filled the air.

The umpire took his time, then yelled at last,

"Yer outta there!"

So as the Mudville players
        swarmed the mound like buzzing bees,
The humbled fans applauded
        Joy's originality.

She proved a girl can play
most any game as well as men.
And yes—you guessed it—
there was joy in Mudville once again.

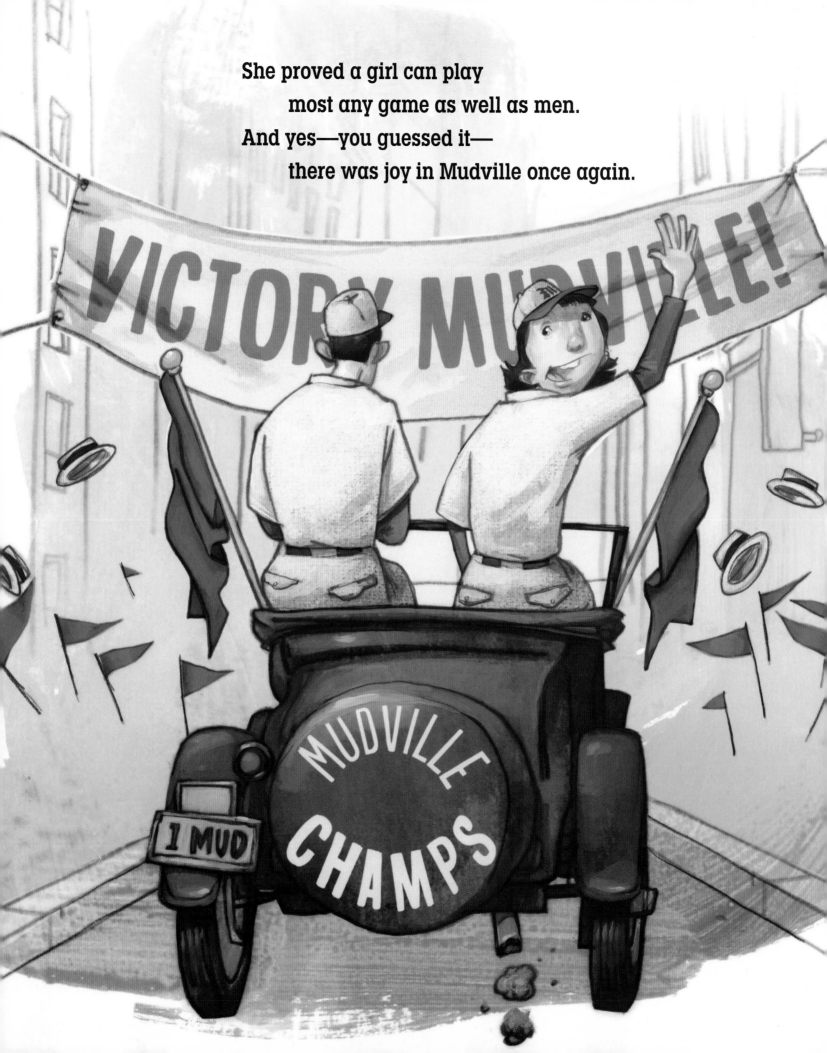

Casey at the Bat

by Ernest Lawrence Thayer

The outlook wasn't brilliant for the Mudville nine that day:
The score stood four to two, with but one inning more to play.
And then when Cooney died at first, and Barrows did the same,
A sickly silence fell upon the patrons of the game.

A straggling few got up to go in deep despair. The rest
Clung to that hope which springs eternal in the human breast;
They thought, if only Casey could get but a whack at that—
We'd put up even money, now, with Casey at the bat.

But Flynn preceded Casey, as did also Jimmy Blake,
And the former was a lulu and the latter was a cake;
So upon that stricken multitude grim melancholy sat,
For there seemed but little chance of Casey's getting to the bat.

But Flynn let drive a single, to the wonderment of all,
And Blake, the much despis-ed, tore the cover off the ball;
And when the dust had lifted, and the men saw what had occurred,
There was Jimmy safe at second and Flynn a-hugging third.

Then from 5,000 throats and more there rose a lusty yell;
It rumbled through the valley; it rattled in the dell;
It knocked upon the mountain and recoiled upon the flat,
For Casey, mighty Casey, was advancing to the bat.

There was ease in Casey's manner as he stepped into his place;
There was pride in Casey's bearing and a smile on Casey's face.
And when, responding to the cheers, he lightly doffed his hat,
No stranger in the crowd could doubt 'twas Casey at the bat.

Ten thousand eyes were on him as he rubbed his hands with dirt;
Five thousand tongues applauded when he wiped them on his shirt.
Then while the writhing pitcher ground the ball into his hip,
Defiance gleamed in Casey's eye, a sneer curled Casey's lip.

And now the leather-covered sphere came hurtling through the air,
And Casey stood a-watching it in haughty grandeur there.
Close by the sturdy batsman the ball unheeded sped—
"That ain't my style," said Casey. "Strike one," the umpire said.

From the benches, black with people, there went up a muffled roar,
Like the beating of the storm-waves on a stern and distant shore.
"Kill him! Kill the umpire!" shouted someone on the stand;
And its likely they'd a-killed him had not Casey raised his hand.

With a smile of Christian charity great Casey's visage shone;
He stilled the rising tumult; he bade the game go on;
He signaled to the pitcher, and once more the spheroid flew;
But Casey still ignored it, and the umpire said, "Strike two."

"Fraud!" cried the maddened thousands, and echo answered fraud;
But one scornful look from Casey and the audience was awed.
They saw his face grow stern and cold, they saw his muscles strain,
And they knew that Casey wouldn't let that ball go by again.

The sneer is gone from Casey's lip, his teeth are clenched in hate;
He pounds with cruel violence his bat upon the plate.
And now the pitcher holds the ball, and now he lets it go,
And now the air is shattered by the force of Casey's blow.

Oh, somewhere in this favored land the sun is shining bright;
The band is playing somewhere, and somewhere hearts are light,
And somewhere men are laughing, and somewhere children shout;
But there is no joy in Mudville—mighty Casey has struck out.

M Mudville

E Squires

ESSEX

COOPERTOWN COSMOS

ST. CROIX

Chicago

GREENV... ...URY

CLEVELAND

Indians